CCer
11/63

S0-ARY-105

To Jonathan Matthew Davies
— B.H.

To Robert, Ben, and Lois from Big Sister
— K.D.

For a free color catalog describing Gareth Stevens' list of high-quality books and multimedia programs, call 1-800-542-2595 (USA) or 1-800-461-9120 (Canada). Gareth Stevens Publishing's Fax: (414) 225-0377.

Library of Congress Cataloging-in-Publication Data

Hooks, William H.
    Mr. Big Brother / by William H. Hooks; illustrated by Kate Duke.
      p. cm. -- (Bank Street ready-to-read)
    Summary: Eli is disappointed when the new baby in his family is a little sister rather than the brother he had expected.
    ISBN 0-8368-2417-2 (lib. bdg.)
    [1. Babies--Fiction. 2. Brothers and sisters--Fiction.] I. Duke, Kate, ill.
II. Title. III. Series.
PZ7.H7664Min 1999
[E]--dc21   99-18573

This edition first published in 1999 by
Gareth Stevens Publishing
1555 North RiverCenter Drive, Suite 201
Milwaukee, Wisconsin 53212 USA

Printed in Mexico

1 2 3 4 5 6 7 8 9 03 02 01 00 99

Bank Street Ready-to-Read™

Mr. Big Brother

by William H. Hooks
Illustrated by Kate Duke

A Byron Preiss Book

Gareth Stevens Publishing
MILWAUKEE

Hi there!
My name is Eli.
But my brother, Jon,
gives me lots of other names.
Like—Mr. Bubble Gum,
     Mr. Monster,
     Mr. Baseball,
     Mr. Dinosaur,
even Mr. Garbage.

Well, it's my turn now.
My mom is going to have a baby.

I'm sure it will be a boy.
I'll be his big brother.
He'll think I'm the greatest!

I'll show him—
    all about blowing bubbles,

how to scare monsters away,

how to hit home runs,

how to make friends
with a dinosaur!

I'll be the tall guy.
And he'll be the small guy.
He'll think I'm Superman!

WOW! Three brothers—
    Big brother Jon,
    Eli, that's me,
    and the new baby.
We'll have—
    our own ball team,
    our own clubhouse,
    our own three-decker bunks!
I won't mind a bit
not being the baby.

I went to sleep dreaming
about my new baby brother.
Dad woke us up the next morning.
"Come on, guys.
Let's go see
the new baby."
"I've already got him
a baseball cap, Dad," I said.

At the hospital
I picked him out right away.
"He looks just like me!" I said.

But Mom said,
"How do you like your new sister?"

"New sister?" I asked.
"Where's my little brother?"
"We have a little girl," said Mom.

I was about to cry.
"Well, take her back.
I want a brother," I said.

That was the worst time
of my life—so far.
I sat on the stoop thinking—
    There goes our ball team,
    and our clubhouse,
    and our three-decker bunks.
16

Mom came out and
put her arms around me,
the way she did when I was little.

Jon's best friend, Roberta, came to see the new baby. Roberta acted real silly, saying "Kootchy-kootchy-koo" to the baby.

My big brother, Jon,
acted just as silly.
"She is SO cute," he said.
"Kootchy-kootchy-koo."

19

They all made such a fuss
over that baby—
Dad,
Mom,
Grandma and Grandpa,
Roberta,
and even Jon.

But not me!
I still wanted a baby brother.

Later Mom said to me,
"Here, Eli, hold the baby."
Just like that,
she put the baby in my lap
and smiled at me.

Before I could say a word,
the telephone rang.
Mom began talking.
I was stuck.

The baby wiggled.
I looked at her face.
And you know what?
She winked at me!
I said, "Hey, you winked at me."
She smiled and winked again.
She kicked her legs
and poked her little hand
right up to my nose.
She IS kind of cute.

25

Just then Jon and Roberta
came in from softball practice.
"Hey, Mr. Garbage," said Jon.
"You make a great baby-sitter!"

It's a good thing
I was holding the baby.
Or we would have had a fight.

Mom said,
"Jon, that was not
a cool thing to say."
Roberta said, "Let me
baby-sit for a while."

Then Jon said,
"Sorry, Little Brother.
Let's go play catch,
just you and me."

While we played,
Jon kept calling me Little Brother.
I said to Jon,
"Don't call me Little Brother.
I'm not little anymore.
You can call me—
    Mr. Big Brother.

And I'll call the baby—
Mr. Sister."

Mr. Sister likes her name.
I can tell.
She smiles and kicks her legs
when I say "Mr. Sister."
And when she grows up,
we can still have—
      our ball team,
      our clubhouse,
      and
      our three-decker bunks!